SWORD AND SORCERY

THE ADVENTURES OF

MERLIN

SWORD AND SORCERY

Text by
Jacqueline Rayner

Based on the stories by
Howard Overman and Julian Jones

BANTAM BOOKS

MERLIN: SWORD AND SORCERY
A BANTAM BOOK 978 0 553 82502 2

First published in Great Britain by Bantam,
an imprint of Random House Children's Books
A Random House Group Company

This edition published 2009

1 3 5 7 9 10 8 6 4 2

The Random House Group Limited supports the Forest Stewardship Council
(FSC), the leading international forest certification organization. All our titles that
are printed on Greenpeace-approved FSC-certified paper carry the FSC logo. Our
paper procurement policy can be found at www.rbooks.co.uk/environment.

Typeset in 16/22 Bembo Schlbk by Falcon Oast Graphic Art Ltd.

Bantam Books are published by Random House Children's Books,
61–63 Uxbridge Road, London W5 5SA

www.**kids**at**randomhouse**.co.uk
www.**rbooks**.co.uk

Addresses for companies within The Random House Group Limited can be found
at: www.randomhouse.co.uk/offices.htm

THE RANDOM HOUSE GROUP Limited Reg. No. 954009

A CIP catalogue record for this book is available from the British Library.

Printed in the UK by CPI Bookmarque, Croydon, CR0 4TD

With grateful thanks to
Johnny Capps, Julian Murphy,
Polly Buckle, Rachel Knight, Sarah Dollard,
Jamie Munro, Pindy O'Brien, Filiz Tosun,
Anna Nettle and Rebecca Morris

CONTENTS

CHAPTER ONE

PERIL IN CAMELOT

The hooded man pulled the young boy closer, trying to keep him safe without revealing how much danger they were in. The city of Camelot was no place for Druids, not when King Uther had banned the use of magic, on penalty of death — but it had the best markets in the kingdom, the only places where certain important supplies could be found.

Pulling his hood further over his face, the

Druid – Cerdan – made his way over to a particular stall. He'd already placed his order for rare herbs and was now returning to collect them. 'Do you have my supplies ready?' he asked the stallholder, a nervous-looking bald man. 'We must leave the city without delay.'

The man reached under his counter and brought out a small bag. 'Everything you asked for – it's all here . . .' he said, handing it over. Then he added, 'I'm sorry.'

It took Cerdan a moment to understand; to recognize the betrayal. His eyes darted all around, searching desperately for an escape route, but guards were coming towards them from both left and right. There was a stone wall behind them; the only way they could go was forward. He ducked under the market stall, dragging the boy after him. The surprised stallholder made no move to stop them, despite the guards' cries of 'Seize them!' Then they ran for their lives.

To Cerdan's horror, their path was leading them not out of the city, but further in. Like sheepdogs herding their flock, the guards were pushing them towards the citadel – the home of Uther himself. As they neared the gates that led to the main square, a guard jumped down on them, his sword catching the boy's arm. The boy screamed ...

. . . and inside the palace, Merlin spun round with a start as he heard a cry – but there was no one there . . .

. . . the guard lifted his sword to deliver the fatal blow. But Cerdan raised a hand and, with an enchantment, threw the swordsman back against the wall.

There were so many guards chasing them now. Escape was surely impossible – they might be able to get into the citadel, but once inside they could never hide and the guards were relentless. Except – perhaps a child on his own might pass unnoticed . . .

Cerdan cast an incantation to pull the citadel gates closed. He pushed the boy towards them as they slowly shut, urging him to run inside − to get through before the way was blocked completely. Then the Druid turned towards the guards, ready to hold them off as long as possible; ready to sacrifice himself so the boy could escape.

Merlin was walking along a corridor when a voice called, *Help!*

He looked around − but he was completely alone. Confused, he carried on, finally leaving the palace and stepping into the main square outside.

Help me.

There were people bustling here and there, but none close enough, none even aware of him. And certainly none who had heard the voice. It was only Merlin who was aware of it. The voice was inside his head.

This wasn't the first time such a thing had happened to him. When Merlin had arrived in Camelot, not that long ago, he had heard a voice summoning him – a voice inside his head which only he could hear.

It turned out that the voice belonged to the Great Dragon. King Uther had imprisoned this beast in the vaults beneath the castle many years before. The Dragon had told the shocked Merlin that he was to become a powerful warlock. His job was to protect Prince Arthur, Uther's son, until Arthur could become a great king. Not that anyone apart from Merlin's mentor, Gaius the physician, was allowed to know all this. To everyone else – including Arthur himself – he remained just the prince's manservant.

Please. You have to help me.

But these cries bore no relation to the deep, sonorous voice of the Dragon. They sounded as if they came from a child.

And there he was – that *had* to be him. A dark-haired, blue-eyed boy of about ten was crouching behind a well, hiding from the crowd. Suddenly Merlin was aware of the guards swarming into the square, hunting high and low. They must be looking for the child, and at this rate it wouldn't be long before they found him.

The boy must be magical, just like Merlin. Perhaps Merlin could speak to him in the same way. It was worth a go. He concentrated on sending words with his mind. *Why are they after you?*

The reply came instantly: *They're going to kill me.*

Not taking his eyes off the boy, Merlin backed into the nearest doorway, shielding

himself as best he could from the searching guards. But they were so close, there was no way to clear a safe path. Their only defences were speed and surprise. *This way*, Merlin called. *Run!*

The boy ran, but he had only taken a few steps before he was spotted. The guards gave chase as he pelted towards Merlin, but the head start was just enough. Merlin grabbed his hand and pulled him though the doorway, into the palace, up the stairs in front of them. But they were in the royal quarters now. The only way out was back the way they'd come, and the guards were coming up behind them. They had to find somewhere to hide, and Merlin could only think of one possibility.

He just had to hope it would be all right . . .

Merlin burst through a door and slammed it behind him. In the room beyond, the king's ward, Morgana, and her maid, Gwen, looked up in surprise.

'Have you forgotten how to knock, Merlin?' Morgana demanded.

He spun round, still instinctively shielding the boy with his arms. 'The guards are after him. I didn't know what to do.'

His heart was pounding. Kind and gentle Gwen would help him without a second

thought, whatever the risk to herself, he knew that. But he was throwing himself on the mercy of Morgana. If she turned against him, it wouldn't only be the boy whose neck would go under the axe.

He stared at her desperately. From behind him came an urgent knock at the door. 'My lady? My lady?'

The guards had caught up with them.

CHAPTER TWO
MORGANA DECIDES

When Morgana was ten years old, her father had been killed fighting for Uther Pendragon, and since coming to live with the king she had seen many people die at his hands. But, unlike Uther, she did not look on each victim as merely a sorcerer or a criminal. She saw them as sons, daughters, brothers, sisters, fathers, mothers. She also witnessed the grief of the loved ones left behind. She did not celebrate at the execution of a so-called traitor; she shared in the pain it caused.

But she had never experienced anything like the emotion she felt as she gazed into the eyes of the Druid boy. She knew she *had* to save him.

For a second she froze as the guards banged on the door, shouting to be let inside. But Morgana was used to being in control and she wasn't fazed for long. 'In there,' she said quickly, pointing to a small alcove screened by heavy curtains. As soon as Merlin and the boy were hidden, she opened the door to the guards and assured them that she had seen nobody.

The instant they had gone she shut the door and locked it. Then she and Gwen hurried over to the alcove. To their horror, they found the boy unconscious – he was losing a lot of blood from a wound to his arm.

Gwen hurried off to gather blankets and pillows to make up some sort of bed for the child. When it was ready, Morgana gently laid him down on it. After a few moments his eyelids began to flicker open, and she was captured once more by his brilliant blue gaze. She couldn't look away. Such a wave of love and compassion surged through her that she felt quite weak and giddy.

But the love brought with it terror too. She had often questioned the king's actions, both behind his back and to his face – but she had never before wilfully defied him in such a way. It was not in Uther's nature to show mercy; he saw them as signs of weakness. Her pleas would not save the boy, and they would not save Merlin or Gwen either, should they be discovered helping to harbour a fugitive. Even she, Uther's ward, would face severe punishment – Morgana was not even convinced that, when it came down to it, her life would be spared. In her mind, she heard the call of the drum that heralded an execution.

Then she realized that the sound was real. Outside her window, Camelot's citizens were indeed being summoned to the main square to witness an execution. Morgana could only hope that the coming days would not see more of them.

Uther did not believe in compassion or mercy, and he did not believe in delay. A magic-user had been captured – there was no need to waste time putting him in the cells or holding a trial. The sooner he lost his head, the better.

It irritated him greatly that his only son, Arthur, questioned his policies. Arthur would one day be king, and what would become of the kingdom if its ruler did not understand how necessary it was to stamp out all magic? Somehow Uther had to get his son to learn this lesson. Now, for instance, Arthur was questioning the necessity of executing the captured Druid, on the grounds that the man had meant no harm. But he used magic – that was harm enough.

'The Druids are peaceful people,' Arthur insisted.

And again Uther had to show the prince how wrong he was. 'Given the chance, they would return magic to the kingdom,' he explained. 'They preach peace but conspire against me. We cannot appear weak.'

'Showing mercy can be a sign of strength,' Arthur said.

The king was appalled. Arthur really didn't understand the realities of government. 'Our enemies will not see it that way. We have a responsibility to protect this kingdom, and executing the Druid will send out a clear message. Now find the boy! Search every inch of the city.'

Arthur seemed reluctant – but at least he would not dare disobey his father, and perhaps he would gain some understanding by following Uther's orders.

For now, Uther had an execution to oversee – and a warning to give.

'People of Camelot. The man before you is guilty of using enchantments and magic, and under our law the sentence for this crime is death. We are still searching for his accomplice. Anyone found harbouring the boy is guilty of conspiracy, and will be executed as a traitor.'

Morgana listened to the king's words with alarm. But nothing would turn her from the path she had chosen. The boy must be protected.

She and Merlin were at the window, watching the Druid being led to the execution block. He showed no fear, not even when addressing the king himself.

'You have let your fear of magic turn to hate,' he said. 'I pity you.'

The man's words would

only serve to strengthen Uther's hostility towards the Druid people, Morgana knew. Their danger increased with every second.

She turned from the window, unable to watch any longer. She gathered the Druid boy to her, wishing she could protect him from the terrible pain of what must happen next.

A shout rose from the crowd outside as the axe fell.

Morgana felt the boy tense, his breathing loud and harsh.

Inside his head, Merlin heard the boy scream in anguish. No sound came from the child's mouth – but the looking glass on the wall suddenly shattered.

Morgana stared at the broken mirror in horror. She had no idea what had just happened.

CHAPTER THREE

QUESTIONS AND CONCERNS

Merlin left the Druid boy with Morgana and returned to the chambers he shared with Gaius. He wouldn't tell the old man what had happened, though – Gaius didn't tend to react well when Merlin got involved in magical matters, especially such dangerous ones.

Although in truth Merlin was beginning to wonder just what he'd got himself into. Not that he regretted his actions; he couldn't have stood and watched as the boy was cut down. But the more he saw the boy, the more worried he became. According to Gaius, it was very rare for children to be born with magic abilities, especially such powerful ones. Someone with Merlin's gifts was, as far as they knew, unique. But yet here was this Druid boy, whose shock and grief had shattered a mirror a dozen feet away.

Merlin waited until he was seated at supper before casually asking, 'Do you know much about the Druids?'

'Very little,' Gaius replied. 'They're very secretive people, especially now they're being hunted by Uther.' The doctor suddenly looked up in alarm, and Merlin saw that his casualness hadn't fooled Gaius. 'Please tell me you haven't got yourself mixed up in this.'

'Me? No. Mixed up in what?'

Gaius fixed him with a hard stare. 'For someone with such a big secret, you are a terrible liar.'

Merlin realized that Gaius wasn't likely to let the matter drop. But he couldn't tell him everything. A lie mixed with just a touch of truth might stop him asking any more questions. 'I heard the boy calling out,' he said. 'He was nowhere to be seen, but I could hear him – like he was inside my mind.'

Gaius nodded thoughtfully. 'Yes, I've heard of this ability. The Druids look for children with such gifts to serve as apprentices.' He gave Merlin a worried glance. 'While they're searching for this boy you must be especially careful, otherwise it will be your head on the chopping block.'

Merlin said, 'I'm always careful. You know me.'

'Yes, Merlin,' replied Gaius in a tone that was hardly reassuring, 'unfortunately I do.'

Merlin waited until Gaius was busy and then headed back to Morgana's rooms, taking some bread with him for the boy. Lady Morgana couldn't be seen to request extra food — it might make the servants curious. As he crossed the square he saw with alarm that the search was still going on: the guards were examining every inch of the castle grounds. Surely they wouldn't dare search the royal chambers — would they?

Morgana welcomed him in and led him to where the boy was sleeping. 'He's very pale,' she said with concern. 'I worry he may have lost a lot of blood.'

'Has he said anything at all?' Merlin asked.

She shook her head. 'Nothing. He won't

even tell me his name.'

They stared down at the child, who tossed restlessly in his sleep. Had they saved him from the axe only to lose him anyway? 'You're taking a huge risk helping the boy,' Merlin said suddenly.

Morgana looked surprised. Like Arthur, she obviously wasn't used to servants being over-familiar. Both tolerated it, though, out of what seemed to be a genuine liking for Merlin. 'I wouldn't see an innocent child executed,' she said. 'What harm has he ever done anyone?'

'Uther believes he has magic, and that makes him guilty,' replied Merlin.

She answered immediately, 'Uther's wrong.'

Merlin was slightly taken aback by her obvious conviction. 'You believe that?'

For a moment Morgana looked almost haunted. 'What if magic isn't something you choose? What if it chooses *you*?' she said. Then, a second later, 'Why are you looking at me like that?'

WHAT IF MAGIC ISN'T SOMETHING YOU CHOOSE?

Merlin realized he was staring and hastily looked away. He was stunned. Morgana couldn't possibly know how right she was – how she had just described his life. He was amazed and pleased that she could feel that way; could understand it so well.

'Why are *you* helping him?' she asked,

and he felt an overwhelming desire to tell her everything – not just how he'd heard the boy speak in his mind, but *everything* – how he was a sorcerer, how he had been born with his powers, the things he could do! He opened his mouth . . .

. . . and said, 'Oh, it was a spur-of-the-moment decision.'

So close. But he mustn't tell her. Gaius was right: he had to be careful.

'What d'you think we should do with him?' Merlin said. 'He can't stay here.'

'We have to find a way to get him back to his people,' she said.

But seeing the way Morgana looked at the boy, Merlin wondered if she would really be able to let him go.

The next day Merlin arrived at Morgana's chambers to find a very worried young woman. She led him to the boy, who was still lying unconscious on the makeshift bed.

'He's burning up,' said Merlin, feeling the boy's forehead. 'How long has he been like this?'

'Since early this morning,' Morgana told him. 'I think his wound may be infected. We have to get him out of Camelot, and we can't do that while he's sick. We need Gaius before it gets any worse.'

But Merlin didn't think that was a good idea. Not just because Gaius would find out that Merlin had been lying, but because his attendance at Morgana's chambers might attract attention. 'I'll treat him,' he announced. 'I'll find out what to do. I'm a fast learner.'

There was a knock at the door, and they looked round in alarm. Morgana jumped up, pulling the curtains across to obscure Merlin and the boy as she left.

'Arthur,' Merlin heard her say as she opened the door. 'To what do I owe this pleasure?'

'Don't get all excited,' came the prince's voice in reply. 'It's not a social call. We're looking for the Druid boy. I'm afraid I'm going to have to search your chambers.'

Merlin listened with horror as Morgana tried to get rid of Arthur, but he insisted on entering. She kept on needling him, obviously hoping that if she annoyed him enough he'd get fed up and leave without searching. It didn't seem to be working, though.

Merlin peeped carefully through the gap in the curtains to see what was happening – and his heart almost stopped. In the middle of the floor were the Druid boy's boots. Any moment now Arthur would spot them, and all would be lost.

CHAPTER FOUR

THE DRAGON'S WARNING

Merlin thought quickly. Quietly he cast a spell, and the boots sprang up, tiptoeing towards the curtained alcove as though a pair of feet were inside them.

Arthur turned towards them. With a gasp, Merlin sent the boots scurrying behind a pillar, where they paused out of sight until the coast was clear. Then they scampered across and came to rest behind the curtains just as the prince finally tired of Morgana's delaying tactics and announced his intention of beginning the search immediately.

'Well, I'll save you the trouble,' she told him. 'The Druid boy's hiding behind the screen.'

Merlin froze in shock. That just wasn't possible. She *couldn't* have said that! And he'd trusted her, brought the boy to her, almost told her his own secret! But a second later her plan became clear.

'I'm sure your father would love to know how you wasted your time by rifling through my things,' she said scornfully. 'Go on.' Would her bluff work, or would it just make Arthur more determined to continue with his search?

'So you can have the satisfaction of making me look like a fool?' he snapped.

'In my experience you don't need any help looking a fool,' she said. 'What are you waiting for? Take a look.'

But Arthur had turned away. 'Why don't you go back to brushing your hair, or whatever it is you do all day,' he said as he strode out of the chamber, slamming the door behind him. Merlin breathed a sigh of relief – very quietly. It wasn't the first time he'd noticed that Morgana seemed able to twist the prince round her little finger.

But although the Druid boy was safe for now, his life was still in great danger – unless Merlin could find a way of curing his infection.

★

It wasn't until night-time that Merlin was able to return to see the boy. Gaius had caught him at his books, and Merlin had had to pretend he had a whole new interest in medicine to stop the physician becoming suspicious. He thought he had the basic idea of what to do though, and he'd mixed up a herbal paste to apply to the wound.

Merlin was kneeling beside the bed while Morgana was off fetching some fresh water when it happened. The boy's eyes flicked open, and a voice inside Merlin's head said, *Thank you, Emrys.*

Merlin stared at him in surprise. He tried again to send a thought back: *Emrys? Why do you call me that?*

Among my people, that is your name.

This was very strange. The Druids knew about him? They even had a special name for him? *You know who I am? How?* the warlock demanded – but the boy had closed his eyes, drifting off into unconsciousness once more.

'Speak to me!' Merlin cried, forgetting to talk with his mind only. But Morgana, returning, took the words at face value.

'I don't know if he *can't* speak, or he's just too scared to,' she said.

Merlin knew the boy could communicate – if he wanted to. It was the other questions that were making the warlock's head reel.

Later that night, Merlin made his way to the Great Dragon's lair, hoping to find some answers.

'No doubt you're here about the Druid boy,' came the creature's surprising greeting.

'How did you know?' Merlin asked.

'Like you, I hear him speak.' Which

perhaps wasn't so odd after all – the Dragon was the only other being Merlin knew who could talk with its mind like that.

The young warlock plunged straight in with his first question. 'Why does he call me Emrys?'

'Because that is your name.'

Merlin shook his head. 'I'm pretty sure my name's Merlin – always has been.'

'You have many names,' boomed the Dragon.

This was getting more confusing by the moment, and Merlin reflected that he'd never known the Dragon not to talk in riddles. He tried again. 'How does the boy know who I am? I've never even met any Druids.'

'There is much written about you that you have yet to read.' Another riddle – of course. But the creature's next words drove it from Merlin's mind. 'You should not protect this boy,' it said.

'Why?' Merlin asked. 'He has magic. He's just like me.'

The Dragon's giant eyes stared down at him. 'You and the boy are as different as day and night.'

'What do you mean?' Merlin demanded.

But spreading out its vast wings, the Dragon soared away. As it vanished into the darkness, its voice floated back: 'Heed my words, Merlin . . .'

CHAPTER FIVE

CONFESSING THE TRUTH

Merlin was reluctant to go to Morgana's rooms the next morning. His conversation with the Dragon had been pounding through his head all night, and he didn't know what to do. He couldn't just abandon the boy – or, rather, he couldn't just abandon Morgana, who was relying on his help. But the Dragon's advice had always seemed to put him on the right path before – well, when he'd worked out what its riddles meant. That was the point, though – surely the Dragon couldn't expect Merlin to heed its words if it wouldn't even explain them properly? So, really, he had to follow his conscience and do his best for the boy.

The trouble was, it seemed that his best wasn't anywhere near good enough. When he arrived, he found Morgana and Gwen doing all they could to nurse the boy, but he was clearly very ill. In the end, Merlin had to give in to Morgana's pleas. He had to ask Gaius for help.

He went to the doctor's rooms. Gaius was hard at work, but Merlin didn't have time to waste waiting for the right moment to break the news. 'Morgana's hiding the Druid boy in her chambers,' he said.

Gaius stopped stock-still. After a few seconds he slowly turned to face Merlin. 'When you say that Morgana's hiding the

Druid boy, I take it that means you're helping her.'

'Sort of,' Merlin admitted.

'You promised me you wouldn't get involved,' said Gaius, sounding furious.

Merlin couldn't help feeling a bit guilty – but what else could he have done? He tried to explain that – and added, 'Are you saying it's wrong to harbour a young magician?' That wasn't fair, but it was true. Gaius wouldn't hand *him* over to Uther; why did he expect Merlin to abandon the Druid boy?

He had to accept the truth of Gaius' answer, though. 'The difference is, Merlin, that your magic is still secret. Although it's a wonder how, considering how careless you are.'

Merlin sighed. He still hadn't told Gaius what he wanted. Summoning up quite a bit of courage, he said, 'The boy's hurt. He's really sick. I've tried to treat him. We need your help.'

'So now you want me to risk *my* neck too,' said the physician. 'I wish the boy no harm, but it's too dangerous.'

'If you don't, we may as well hand him over to the guards, because he'll die anyway.'

This really wasn't fair. He was trying to force Gaius to help them against his will, trying to make him do something he really didn't want to do. But Merlin didn't feel he had any choice. He had to try one last time. 'You didn't turn your back on me. Please don't turn your back on him.'

A short time later, Gaius knelt beside the Druid boy's bed. Morgana hovered by his side, anxiously awaiting the doctor's verdict. But she knew that he would help. How could he not, when he saw how much this child meant to her? The child had even, at last, spoken her name . . . It was true that Gwen had claimed to hear nothing, but Morgana had heard the word quite clearly – almost as if it had arrived directly in her head.

'I will treat the boy,' Gaius said eventually, 'but as soon as he is well, you must get him out of Camelot.'

Morgana didn't argue. She knew it was too dangerous for the boy to stay. But, inside, the thought was tearing her apart.

Gaius drew back the rough bandage on the boy's arm. 'Well,' he said with a grimace, 'one thing we know for certain.'

'What's that?' Merlin asked.

The doctor gave him a wry smile. 'You're no physician.'

They were all agreed – they had to get the boy out of Camelot as soon as possible. But it wasn't going to be easy: the guards were searching everyone leaving the palace. However, Merlin knew of a secret door in the armoury that led to the lower town, past the guard posts, and offered to take him out that way.

Morgana refused to hear of it. She would be the one to smuggle the boy out. The big problem they then had was getting hold of the key to the armoury door. There was only one key – and Prince Arthur had it.

★

That evening, Merlin brought Arthur's evening meal to his room. He was a bit worried he'd been neglecting his duties and didn't want the prince to suspect anything – but that wasn't the main reason he waited on Arthur so attentively. There on the prince's belt hung all the keys to the castle: several small bunches of keys all attached to a large metal ring. The ones to the armoury door hung temptingly near a break in the ring.

Merlin placed a bowl of soup in front of the prince and retreated to a convenient position just behind him. Then, with a softly whispered spell, he caused the keys to slip off the ring and float towards him. Suddenly Arthur turned round to ask for bread – but as quick as thought, Merlin made the keys jump behind the prince's head.

Too quick. The flying keys jangled together, and the puzzled prince looked for

the source of the noise. 'What was that?' he asked.

'What?' asked Merlin innocently, trying to keep the keys just out of the prince's sight.

'There was a sound . . .' Arthur looked around, trying to trace the noise. As he turned left, the keys went right. As he turned right, the keys went left. As he looked up, the keys dropped down.

'I think I saw something over there,' Merlin said, pointing to the far side of the room. Arthur hurried over to investigate, and the warlock gratefully gave up his magical hold on the keys. They fell into the soup bowl.

'What was that?' Arthur came back over. 'There was a different sound – like a splash.'

Merlin shook his head. 'I didn't hear anything,' he said. Arthur was clearly getting annoyed now, and the warlock hoped he'd want to get away from the strange noises – and his infuriating servant – rather than finish his meal.

To Merlin's great relief, the prince made one more attempt to locate the source of the noise, and then left the room. A minute later, with the soupy keys safely in his pocket, Merlin was on his way too.

CHAPTER SIX
ESCAPE TO DANGER

Gwen lived in the lower town; she could easily return home from the palace, and the guards wouldn't stop Merlin leaving to pay her a visit. Morgana would take the Druid boy through the castle to the armoury, avoiding all the corridors usually patrolled by guards. Once through the secret door, they would make their way to Gwen's house, where horses and supplies would be waiting.

'Morgana really cares about the boy,'

Gwen said to Merlin as they waited anxiously for the others to arrive. 'I've never seen her this way with anyone.'

'I'm sure she just wants to protect him,' said Merlin. Of course he wasn't sure at all, but he didn't want to worry Gwen with his own fears about Morgana's obsessive attachment. He almost made a joke about the boy casting a spell on her, but caught himself just in time.

He would have felt even less like joking had he known what was happening inside the palace. Morgana had done her best to keep out of sight – but a servant had spotted her and the boy entering the armoury and hurried off to raise the alarm. The two fugitives made it through the secret door, along the tunnel behind it and out into the town, but just as Merlin spotted them from the window, the warning bell began to peal.

Morgana and the boy hurried into the house. Gwen handed over a bag. 'There's enough food for three days,' she said.

'Your horse is fed and watered,' Merlin added. 'I'll take you to it.'

'No,' said Morgana. 'There's no point all of us risking our lives. I'm the king's ward. I'll take my chances.'

'Morgana ...' Gwen protested. Merlin knew how much she cared for her mistress.

But Morgana was firm. 'I couldn't live with myself if anything happened to either of you.' She hadn't let go of the boy's hand for a second. Now she pulled him towards her. 'We must go.'

She opened the door. As the boy followed her out, his eyes caught Merlin's, and the warlock almost took a step back, away from the force of that gaze. *Goodbye, Emrys*, came a voice in his head.

Merlin shivered, relieved that the child was leaving at last.

Morgana led the boy towards the stables. They had almost made it when, to her horror, she heard a great thump of footsteps. A troop of guards came into view, Arthur at its head.

Terrified, she ran towards a nearby grain store and pulled the child behind a pile of sacks. Her breath was coming fast; surely it could be heard from miles away.

The door to the grain store opened, and she heard Arthur ordering his men to fan out. The guards had flaming torches – they were shining them into every corner.

She hugged the boy to her. They would have to kill her before she would let them have him.

But as the guards raised their torches, Morgana spotted something in the light. There was a door at the other end of the shed! It was their only chance . . .

Quietly, carefully, no longer even daring to breathe, she crept out from the hiding place, pulling the boy behind her. Quietly, carefully, they hurried across the floor. The door! There it was! They'd made it!

As they took their last few steps, a guard appeared in front of them. Then another.

Morgana gasped and began to back

away. She was gripping the boy so tightly she must have caused him pain, but still he made no sound.

She stopped as a sword point touched the back of her neck. 'Halt or I'll run you through,' said a voice.

Arthur's voice.

Morgana turned. She had never seen the prince looked so shocked.

They fought and quarrelled, they teased and nagged, but for a decade they had been like brother and sister. However they might act most of the time, underneath they cared deeply for each other. Morgana had no hope now but for Arthur's mercy,

and for this child she would beg, she would grovel, she would throw herself to the ground for Arthur to walk on – she would do anything. 'Let him go,' she entreated him, putting everything she could into her plea. 'I beg you. He's just a child.'

He would have helped her – perhaps. But the guards were there, watching. So it was with much heartache but little surprise that she heard him give the order: 'Restrain them.'

CHAPTER SEVEN

THE CRUELTY
OF THE KING

'All this time you've been hiding the boy – in my own palace!' shouted Uther. 'How could you betray me like this?'

Morgana faced the furious king with dignity. 'I would not see him executed,' she said.

'I've treated you like a daughter. Is this how you repay me?'

But she knew that Uther was no parent to her. A parent would feel about their child like she felt about the Druid boy. A parent would understand her actions. A parent would cast no blame. 'I did what I thought was right,' she said.

That angered him even more. 'You think it is right to conspire with my enemies against me?'

'How could this child be your enemy?' she cried. 'He's just a boy!'

'He's a Druid. His kind would see me dead and this kingdom return to anarchy, and you would help them.'

Behind Uther, Arthur stood with his head bowed. He seemed uncomfortable, but Morgana had no sympathy to spare for him. If he had let her go – well, Uther would have punished him, of course, perhaps harshly. But the king wouldn't execute his own son. Whereas the Druid boy's life was now forfeit, and his blood would be on Arthur's hands too.

She knew that Uther would never listen to her arguments. Once again, her only chance was to plead for mercy. 'Then punish me. But spare the boy, I beg you.'

But once again, her plea failed.

Uther turned to Arthur. 'Make arrangements for the boy to be executed tomorrow morning.'

'No!' Morgana screamed. The child could not die, he could not be taken from her. She had thought she understood the agony

MAKE ARRANGEMENTS FOR THE BOY TO BE EXECUTED TOMORROW MORNING.

NO!

of the parents who had watched Uther sentence their children to death; thought that, through her sympathy, she had shared their pain. She had been an ignorant fool. This pain was like nothing else in the world; she had never felt the smallest part of it before. 'Please,' she entreated. 'He has done nothing.'

But all Uther said was, 'Let this be a lesson to you,' before turning to leave.

And that was the worst thing of all – that the king, in his cruelty, was killing the boy to punish her. Suddenly she was filled with contempt for the man. He was not worthy to rule a village, let alone a kingdom. She stood up straight. Her pleas had not worked; there was nothing she could say to make a difference, so it didn't matter what she said. 'What have these people done to you?' she cried, running after the king. 'Why are you so full of hate?'

Uther spun round and his hand fastened around Morgana's neck. She froze in shock. 'Enough!' he shouted. 'I will not hear another word. Do not speak to me until you are ready to apologize for what you've done.' He shoved the girl away and she stumbled backwards.

She stared after him as he left the room, hardly able to believe that he'd treated her like that. In her whole life, no one had ever raised a hand to her before.

Arthur followed his father and Morgana looked at him with hatred too. He hadn't even said one word in her defence – and he was just going to stand back and let Uther kill the Druid boy.

Arthur hurried to catch up with his father. Morgana would have been surprised to hear what he had to say.

'Perhaps imprisonment is a more suitable

punishment for the boy,' he suggested. 'He's so young.' Morgana's words had made an impression on Arthur, but that was not his main reason for speaking. Nor was it guilt at being the one who had captured the child – he was enough of a realist to know that no other course of action had been open to him. What drove him to speak up was a genuine belief that no child deserved to die for choices it hadn't made. He knew that convincing his father of that would be an impossible task; nevertheless, he had to try.

Uther dismissed his words angrily. 'It would allow him to grow more powerful, more dangerous, until he strikes against us,' he said.

'We don't know he's going to strike against us,' said Arthur. 'He's yet to do anything!'

'It is enough that his people conspire to

overthrow me. This is harsh, but necessary. I take no pleasure in killing the boy.'

'Then spare him for Morgana's sake!' the prince cried. 'She's clearly grown attached to the boy, and if you execute him I fear she will never forgive you.'

The king stopped and turned on his son,

 his eyes blazing. 'I do not seek her forgiveness! She has betrayed me.'

Arthur knew he was treading on very dangerous ground, but still he said, 'Yet you're sparing her?'

Uther took a deep breath. 'She has the promise I made her father to thank for that. The boy enjoys no such privilege. He *will* be killed at dawn. Is that clear?'

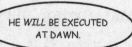

HE *WILL* BE EXECUTED AT DAWN.

★

Arthur headed back to his chambers, deeply troubled. Uther was not only his father but his king, and he could not disobey him. And yet everything in him was crying out that he could not let the child be killed.

He was not happy to find Morgana in his room. Despite all the sympathy he felt for her, he was very angry. He was in this impossible situation because of her, and she had lied to him too.

'You can't let your father execute the boy,' she said as he walked in.

'You're lucky he's not executing *you*!' Arthur replied, his anger spilling out. 'Are you telling me he really *was* behind the screen when I came to search your chambers?'

He knew the answer already, and sure enough, she nodded. But even in the face of his fury, she persisted with her pleas.

'I know you believe your father's wrong to execute him. We have to get the boy back to his people.'

'Forget it,' he said, astonished she'd ask for his help under such circumstances.

Morgana flushed with anger as she snapped, 'I can't believe you'd let an innocent child die!'

Why wouldn't she even try to understand? This was not his doing and not his choice. 'It's too late. He's been caught. There's nothing I can do about it.'

'And this is how you will rule when you are king?'

Her words cut into him. He did not wish to rule in this way, but that meant nothing. Here and now, he was not the ruler – and he could not betray his father, the king.

Morgana's voice softened. 'If I know you at all, you won't stand by and let this happen. Please. If you won't do this for the boy, then do it for me.'

Arthur couldn't disobey his father. Yet could he let down Morgana instead?

CHAPTER EIGHT
A NEW PLAN

If Morgana were to be captured, would she betray them? That had been Merlin's worry as he and Gwen had waited anxiously for news. Finally gossip had filtered through to them that the Druid boy had been found – and that must mean that Morgana had been caught too. So what would happen now? What would happen to Merlin and Gwen? It wasn't that Merlin didn't trust Morgana, not really; but he'd seen how she was with the boy. If there was a way she could save his life by handing them over – well, Merlin wasn't entirely sure that she wouldn't.

Finally he couldn't bear the suspense any longer. He had to go back to the palace to find out what had happened to Morgana, and if the guards were waiting for him, then so be it. He couldn't skulk around in Gwen's house for ever.

But the guards showed no interest in him as he wandered through the gates and went up to Morgana's rooms. He was slightly surprised to find her there – he'd half expected her to be locked in the dungeons – but of course he was pleased. He was less pleased, though, when she once again asked him to help the Druid boy.

But the boy was in gaol! Merlin didn't think there was anything he could do; didn't know if he *wanted* to do anything.

Morgana hadn't handed him over to Uther, though, so he felt he had to agree. But was it the right thing to do?

She left her chambers, and Merlin wandered around for a while just thinking, but no answers came to him. In the end he set off for Arthur's rooms. The prince was bound to have a load of jobs for him, and at least that would keep his mind off things.

Merlin was out of luck. When he got to Arthur's chambers, he found Morgana there.

Arthur didn't seem very pleased to see him. 'Sorry, was I interrupting something?'

Merlin asked, happy for an excuse to get out of there.

However, Morgana beckoned him in. 'I trust Merlin,' she said.

This didn't sound good. It seemed that more plans were afoot. But Merlin certainly didn't expect Arthur's next words: 'We're going to break the Druid boy out of the dungeons.'

'It's too dangerous!' Merlin cried. But although he was horrified, his admiration for Arthur grew further. He knew it took a lot for the prince to defy his father. He'd done it once before to save Merlin's life, when his servant had been poisoned by the

WE'RE GOING TO BREAK THE DRUID BOY OUT OF THE DUNGEONS.

sorceress Nimueh, but now he was crossing him for a boy he scarcely knew. Merlin reflected once again that Arthur was going to make a great king. Mind you, he might spend the time until his coronation locked up in gaol. Uther wasn't going to be at all happy with his son.

The danger was even greater for Morgana though. 'You've already been caught once. And if the king catches you a second time, he'll never forgive you,' Merlin told her.

'I'm not worried for myself,' she replied.

But Arthur was nodding. 'Merlin's right. When my father finds out the boy's escaped he'll suspect you of being involved.' He thought for a second. 'You must go to him and apologize. Dine with him. He cannot hold you responsible if you are with him when the boy escapes.'

'You need me if the plan is to work,' said Morgana. 'You can't do this on your own.'

'Merlin will take your place,' said the prince.

'Me?' Merlin wondered if things could get any worse.

Arthur explained. 'I'm going to take the boy out through the burial vaults. There's a tunnel that leads beyond the city walls. Get my horse and meet me there. There's a grate that covers the entrance to the tunnel. Bring a rope and a grappling hook to pull it off.'

Merlin opened his mouth to protest, but Arthur continued. 'Merlin, do you understand? If you're not there to meet us, we will surely be caught.'

So what could Merlin do but agree?

He was deeply troubled, though. Arthur was involved now – Arthur, whom he had to protect at all costs. The Dragon had told him that. But the Dragon had also told him to abandon the Druid boy. Merlin could not obey both the Dragon's commands: now he was being pulled in two different directions. He had to understand more – he had to know why the Dragon insisted he shouldn't protect the boy.

He would visit it again, and this time he wouldn't leave until it had given him a proper answer.

'I need to know why you told me not to protect the Druid boy!' Merlin shouted into the darkness.

The Dragon landed in front of him. 'You seek my counsel and yet you choose to ignore it.'

Merlin was in no mood to accept the Dragon's recriminations. If the creature wanted him to follow its advice, it had to explain things better. 'Just tell me *why*,' he said.

'If the boy lives, you cannot fulfil your destiny and Arthur will die,' it replied.

The warlock was stunned; for a moment he couldn't speak. His thoughts raced round his head as he wondered how the boy could possibly bring about Arthur's death. Some terrible accident? Revenge of the Druids for the persecution they had suffered under Uther? One terrible conclusion leaped into his mind, but he could hardly believe it. He had to ask, though. 'You don't mean that little boy's going to kill Arthur . . . ?'

'It seems that is up to you. You have it in your power to prevent a great evil,' said the Dragon.

Merlin couldn't take it all in. 'No,' he said. 'You can't know that for certain. The future isn't set in stone.'

The Dragon stared at him. 'You must let the boy die.'

Merlin had got what he came for – a proper answer. And he didn't like it one bit.

CHAPTER NINE

THE BEGINNING OF THE END

As Gwen dressed her, Morgana readied herself for the role she would have to play. There had been times when she had found it hard to conceal her true feelings, but those outbursts had come in the heat of the moment. This time she would remain calm. She was prepared; she knew what she had to do. She would pretend to be Uther's dutiful ward, and not let her hatred show.

She noticed Gwen looking at her, worry

creasing the girl's brow. 'What is it? What's wrong?' she said.

Her maid hesitated, then said, 'You're risking so much for this boy. You don't know anything about him. You don't even know his name.'

Morgana did not like her actions to be questioned, but she knew Gwen was motivated by concern for her. And although she would not let her thoughts dwell on the matter, she realized deep down inside that Gwen had a point. It was true that she knew nothing about the boy.

All she knew was that if he died, a large part of her would die with him. 'There is a bond between us,' she said.

'Stronger than the bond you have with Uther?' said Gwen.

Yes. Because there was no longer a bond. Uther had broken it when he took the child from her. 'It's like nothing I've ever felt before,' she said. 'Perhaps I was always meant to help him . . .' Even as she said it, she realized she didn't know quite what she meant. But there was no time to consider it further. She had to go to Uther.

She would weep. She would apologize. But she would mean none of it.

Arthur had used a smoke device made from burning herbs to knock the guards unconscious; a trick he'd learned many years ago from a grizzled old warrior who liked to gain every advantage in battle. He'd wondered if the old man had been making up stories, and was relieved to discover that it did actually work. But he didn't know how long the men would stay asleep, so he had to hurry.

He made his way to the cell and unlocked the door. The boy looked alarmed, although he made no sound. 'Don't be scared,' the prince told him. 'I've sent word to your people. I'm taking you to them. You must come with me.'

Arthur held out a hand and the boy took it. Together, they ran.

They made it right to the end of the secret tunnel before the alarm was raised.

Arthur was worried, but he knew Merlin would be there to open the grille. They could still get away.

But when they reached it, Merlin wasn't there.

In his bedroom, Merlin heard the alarm
bell. Guilt threatened to overwhelm him.
Arthur would be caught. Arthur would
never trust him again. Arthur would be
punished. But another thought knocked
those aside: at least Arthur would be alive.

Coming to this decision had been
almost impossible. How could he let
such a terrible thing happen, even to stop
something worse happening in the future?
Allowing the Druid boy to die was awful;
but allowing Arthur to die, the man who
was to be such a great king – that was
unthinkable.

And to stop that happening, Merlin didn't have to do a thing. He just had to . . . do nothing.

Where are you, Emrys? The boy's voice pierced his mind.

Merlin ignored it. But he felt like he was sharpening the executioner's axe himself.

Emrys! Help us. Please. I'm scared, Emrys. Don't do this. They'll kill me. I know you can hear me. I thought you were my friend. We're the same! I don't want to die. Emrys! Emrys! Emrys!

And it was Merlin's arms that brought down the axe with a *thud*.

He couldn't do it. He couldn't let the child die. Somehow he would change the future that the Dragon predicted. He had to solve the problem he saw now – the future would come later.

★

'Where have you been?' Arthur demanded angrily as Merlin ran up to the grille.

'I had trouble getting out of the castle,' he replied shortly.

'Well, get this grate off. The guards are coming!'

The warlock quickly attached the grappling hook to the grate and let Arthur's horse pull it away. Within seconds Arthur and the boy had scrambled through the hole and were mounting the horse.

'If my father asks where I am, I've gone on a hunting trip,' Arthur called back. 'Better make yourself scarce or they'll execute you in his place.'

But Merlin found it hard to move. The enormity of what he'd done was hitting home. A voice inside his head said, *Goodbye, Emrys. I know that someday we will meet again.* As he watched the boy vanish into the distance, Merlin hoped that day would never come.

How could it ever be that this child would come to destroy the man who had risked so much to save him?

Morgana had wept. She had apologized humbly. Uther had forgiven her. And for the rest of the evening she hadn't left Uther's sight.

When she heard the alarm bell, she had tried to look only mildly concerned.

When the guard rushed in to inform the king of the Druid boy's escape, she had concealed her joy.

But Uther had been a king for many years, and she had dangerously underestimated him. 'If I discover that you were somehow involved in freeing this boy, the consequences will be extremely severe,' he said, his expression almost condemning her to death already.

'My lord,' she said artfully, 'you know I

respect you too much to ever betray you like that.'

He leaned towards her, and when he spoke, each word was like a blow. 'I made a promise to your father that I would protect you. But if you cross me again, I will break that promise without a second thought.'

He strode from the room, leaving Morgana shaken – and more full of hatred than ever.

The Druids were waiting in the forest. Arthur helped the boy down from his horse and led him towards them.

'We are for ever indebted to you, Arthur Pendragon, for returning the boy to us,' said one, taking the boy's hand.

'You must not let it be known that it was I who brought him to you,' the prince told them.

The man nodded. 'You have my word.'

They turned to leave.

Suddenly a thought struck Arthur. 'Wait!' he called after the boy. 'I don't even know your name!'

The boy turned, but said nothing. He looked up at his companion, as if seeking permission. The older Druid nodded.

'My name is Mordred,' said the Druid boy.

Arthur smiled. 'Good luck, Mordred,' he said.

For the first time since entering Camelot, the boy smiled.

It was a smile that Arthur would never forget.

CHAPTER TEN
THE DEAD WAKE

For weeks after the Druid boy's escape, Merlin had been able to think of little but Arthur's future, going over his actions again and again. Had he done the right thing? Had he made a terrible mistake?

He would not have spent so much time reliving the past or worrying about the distant future if he had realized that, in the present, someone was even now planning a terrible revenge – a revenge that might cost the prince his life.

In the crypts below Camelot a witch searched for a tomb. Merlin would have recognized the beautiful young woman, because he had met her before. In reality, though, she was neither young nor beautiful; she used enchantment to disguise herself. Her name was Nimueh, and on her last visit to Camelot she had tried to poison Merlin. If Arthur hadn't risked his own life to obtain an antidote, the young warlock would have died.

She found the tomb she sought. Calling on the forces of dark magic, she intoned a terrible spell.

Under her hands, the coffin lid began to crack.

Arthur had come of age now; should it become necessary, he could rule the kingdom with no need for advisers or guardians. His coming of age was marked by the ceremony naming him Crown Prince of Camelot.

Merlin felt a swell of pride as Arthur knelt before the king and swore a solemn oath to protect the people of Camelot and rule them well. Of course, he wasn't going to *admit* to feeling like that. He didn't want anyone to think he was getting soft or beginning to enjoy being Arthur's servant. He might admire the prince hugely for his bravery and nobility,

but Arthur was still the man who ordered Merlin around and made him wash the royal socks and things like that. Anyway, Arthur had enough people fawning over him already. Just look at all those knights and courtiers cheering him as he paraded in front of them in his shiny new crown.

Suddenly the cheers turned to screams.

Everyone in the court spun round in shock as a black-armoured knight on horseback smashed through the vast stained-glass window at the end of the great hall.

Arthur drew his sword. The rest of the knights of

Camelot did likewise as the mounted figure rode slowly towards the king.

The horse stopped. The knight pulled off one black metal gauntlet and flung it to the floor – the knightly way of issuing a challenge to combat. Merlin had been with Arthur long enough to know that the knight's code did not allow such a challenge to be ignored.

The prince sheathed his sword, ready to pick up the gauntlet – but before he could do so, the man by his side had stepped forward. 'I, Sir Owain, accept your challenge!' cried the young knight, holding the metal glove aloft.

The Black Knight turned to Owain. He did not remove his helmet as he declared his terms. 'Single combat. Noon tomorrow. To the death.'

As the knight turned his horse, Merlin spotted the shield he wore on his arm: it bore the crest of a silver eagle. He also caught sight of Gaius' face. The old doctor looked as though he'd seen a ghost.

Merlin wouldn't stop asking questions.

He and Gaius were back in the doctor's chambers and the doctor was trying to get on with some work to distract himself from the terrible memories now crowding into his head. But Merlin went on and on: 'Have you ever seen this Black Knight before? Did you recognize his crest? Do you think he's from around here? What's he doing here?' Gaius gave noncommittal, and probably unconvincing, answers. In the end he ordered the young warlock to bed.

As soon as Merlin was out of the way, Gaius left the room. He couldn't rest until he'd visited the Hall of Records and consulted his old friend Geoffrey of Monmouth, one of the few people who had been at court as long as Gaius had – one of the few people who had witnessed long-ago events that were never now spoken of.

'Gaius, thank God,' Geoffrey exclaimed as the doctor entered.

'You know why I'm here?' Gaius asked.

The other nodded. 'The Black Knight. You saw his crest?'

'Yes.' Gaius pointed to the book of heraldry open on the desk. 'Have you confirmed it?'

'It is the crest of Tristan du Bois,'

said Geoffrey. 'No other knight has ever carried it.'

It was the answer Gaius both expected and feared. But what he must do now made him even more afraid. He had to tell the king.

He made his way to the council chambers where Uther sat alone. The king seemed lost in thought, and Gaius suspected he already knew what the doctor was going to say.

'What is it?' Uther demanded as he entered.

Gaius wasted no time. 'The knight, sire. He bears the crest of Tristan du Bois.'

The king nodded. 'Yes.'

'But he's been dead for twenty years.'

'I know,' said Uther. 'I killed him.' He looked Gaius straight in the eye. 'Dead men do not return.' And the doctor knew that any further conversation was pointless.

DEAD MEN DO NOT RETURN.

Outside the castle, by the gates of Camelot, the Black Knight stood and waited. A lone dark sentinel who did not move until dawn.

CHAPTER ELEVEN
FIGHT TO THE DEATH

Noon arrived so quickly the next day. One minute Merlin was helping Owain on with his armour, listening to Arthur trying to pretend everything was going to be fine; the next, or so it seemed, they were entering the tournament ground.

'Remember,' said the prince as they bade Owain farewell, 'all it takes to kill a man is one well-aimed blow. Find the flow of the fight and try to control it. I've watched you fight and I know no one better.'

Everyone was assembled to watch the fight. The king was there, of course, with Morgana by his side, and Merlin also spotted Gaius' worried face in the crowd.

The Black Knight had been on horseback the evening before and his size had been hard to judge. It was not until Owain approached him, both now on foot, that Merlin realized how huge the man was. He towered above his opponent. Their only hope was that he was less skilled than the Knight of Camelot.

Arthur took his place by King Uther. 'Let battle commence,' Uther announced.

Neither knight held back. Blow after blow rained down, all blocked with shield or sword. To Merlin's relief, Owain seemed to be holding his own — perhaps even gaining the advantage at times. Yes, Owain definitely had his opponent on the back foot! As Merlin watched, the young knight seized his chance. 'One well-aimed blow!' Arthur called from the stands, and there it was – Owain ran his sword through the Black Knight's chest.

Merlin cheered. But to his amazement, no one else took up the cry. What was wrong? Hadn't they seen what had happened? And why hadn't the Black Knight fallen?

As Merlin looked on, amazed, the fight continued. Now Owain was being beaten backwards. Now the Black Knight had knocked him to the ground. Now the Black Knight raised his sword . . .

The crowd gasped in horror.

Owain was dead.

The Black Knight turned and approached the royal family. As he stopped he pulled off his gauntlet, then flung it on the ground. 'Who will take up my challenge?' he snarled.

Without a second's hesitation, Arthur rose from his seat. Almost as quickly, Uther's arm shot out and pulled him back. As the prince spun round to confront his father, another knight jumped down into the arena. 'I, Sir Pellinor, take up the challenge!' he cried.

'So be it,' the knight replied. But as he turned to leave, it was not Pellinor he was looking at, but Uther.

'Should we tend to his wounds?' Merlin said to Gaius as the Black Knight passed them. It wasn't that he cared if the knight was hurt – but it was part of the rules.

Gaius looked surprised, though. 'Owain didn't land a blow.'

'He did,' Merlin insisted.'I saw it – Owain's sword definitely pierced him.' He wondered then if he had only seen the blow because of his magical abilities – for him, time could slow down. Usually it was deliberate and he could control it, but perhaps as he had been concentrating so hard it had happened all by itself. Anyway, he knew that he hadn't imagined it. 'He should be dead,' he said.

The doctor's answer came as a shock. 'Perhaps he already is.'

★

'Are you sure we should be doing this?' Merlin said that night as he followed Gaius into the burial vaults below the palace.

'You're not scared, are you?' said the doctor.

Merlin shook his head. 'No, I love old crypts. I wouldn't be seen dead anywhere else!'

Gaius was not amused.

Behind them, the door suddenly slammed shut, plunging them into darkness. 'Must've been a gust of wind,' Gaius said. They stood frozen in the gloom, not knowing where to put their feet. 'We should have brought a torch.'

With a swift spell, Merlin lit a torch on the wall. 'Handy!' Gaius commented. The warlock grinned. Magic did come in very useful.

Gaius knew what he was looking for.

'Bring the torch over here,' he said, pointing towards a tomb.

Merlin felt uneasy. 'We're breaking into someone's grave?' he asked.

'No,' said Gaius as the torchlight illuminated the shattered stone of the coffin lid and the void beyond, 'we're too late. I think someone's already broken out.'

Back in Gaius' chambers, the doctor hurried to his bookshelves and began to sort through the volumes there.

'So the tomb belongs to Tristan du Bois,' Merlin said. 'But who is he?'

'He was the brother of Ygraine, Uther's wife — Arthur's mother,' Gaius explained. 'She died giving birth to Arthur, and Tristan blamed Uther. He came to the gates of Camelot and challenged the king to single combat. Uther won. But with his dying breath, Tristan cursed Camelot to one day suffer his return.' Gaius found a book and brought it over to the table. 'I thought it was the ramblings of a dying man.'

'Men don't just rise up from the dead, though,' said Merlin, 'no matter how angry they are.'

But Gaius had located the page he wanted. He pointed to the illustration of a skeletal knight. 'It's my guess we're dealing with a wraith. The spirit of a dead man conjured from the grave.'

Merlin was shocked. 'So this is the work of a sorcerer?'

The doctor nodded. 'Powerful magic can harness the grief and rage of a tormented soul and make it live again.'

'How do we stop it?' Merlin asked.

'We can't.' Gaius looked grim. 'Because it is no longer alive, no mortal weapon can kill it. Nothing can stop it until it has achieved what it came for – revenge on Camelot.'

'What does that mean for Sir Pellinor?' said Merlin.

Gaius sighed. 'I'm afraid it doesn't look good.'

Arthur was also worried about Sir Pellinor – and he was furious with the king for preventing him from taking up the challenge.

Uther had tried to calm him down. 'We have to give our knights a chance to prove themselves,' he insisted. 'And Sir Pellinor is more than a match for this stranger.'

The prince wasn't convinced. 'He's still not recovered from the wounds he suffered at Ethandun. You're sending him to his death!'

'It was his choice to take up the gauntlet,' said Uther. 'I am not to blame.'

Arthur had the strangest feeling that the king, usually so sure, was trying to convince himself of that.

Outside the castle, the Black Knight stood once more by the gates of Camelot, waiting silent and still for the dawn.

Chapter Twelve

The Gauntlet Is Thrown

Sir Pellinor had two advantages over Sir Owain: he was a more experienced warrior and he had seen the Black Knight fight before.

As the fight began, to the delight of the crowd, the Black Knight seemed to be on the defensive. Again and again Pellinor thrust his sword at the stranger, and only with an effort were his blows parried. The knight responded with heavy swings of his massive two-handed sword, but Pellinor defended himself expertly with shield and blade.

Then came the moment the crowd had been hoping for. Pellinor used his shield to push aside the two-handed sword, and the stranger's stomach was unguarded. The young knight pushed his sword home. This time everyone saw the blade go in.

But the knight did not fall, and history repeated itself. Pellinor had stepped back, sure of his victory. He did not expect the Black Knight to fight on. He had no time to defend himself from the killing blow.

As the crowd gasped in shock, the stranger once again turned towards the royal family

– but before he could issue his challenge, a gauntlet fell at his feet. A gauntlet emblazoned with the golden Dragon of the Pendragons.

Uther looked up in horror as his son stood and addressed the Black Knight. 'I, Arthur Pendragon, challenge you. Single combat. Noon tomorrow.'

The knight showed no emotion. 'So be it,' he said.

'How could you be so stupid?' Uther shouted at his son when they were alone. 'I will revoke the challenge!'

'No.' Arthur's voice was cold. 'The knight's code must be upheld. That's what you told me. Once a challenge has been laid down you cannot rescind it.'

'This is different – you are Crown Prince!' said Uther.

The prince shook his head. 'There cannot be one rule for me and one for all the rest.'

Uther was desperate. 'I forbid you to fight.'

'You want me to prove that I'm worthy of the throne,' said Arthur. 'I cannot do that by being a coward.'

'No, Arthur, this will be your death!'

Arthur turned to leave. 'I'm sorry you have so little faith in me, Father.'

The king called after his son, but the prince kept walking, leaving his father in despair. It was not a question of faith, but of certainty. Arthur could beat any mortal man in combat, Uther was sure of that. But he also knew, though he shrank from admitting it, that the Black Knight was no mortal man.

★

Gaius and Merlin shared the king's worries. 'If Arthur fights that thing, he'll die,' Merlin said after they returned to Gaius' chambers.

'He is Camelot's strongest warrior,' Gaius said. 'If anyone can defeat it, he can.'

Merlin shook his head. 'You said yourself, no mortal weapon can kill it. Which means we have to find a way to defeat the wraith ourselves.' He crossed over to the stairs that led to his room.

'How do you propose to do that?' said the doctor.

'If no mortal sword will kill it,' Merlin called back as he disappeared upstairs, 'then I will . . . With mortal magic,' he added as he came back down again, his magic book under his arm.

He began to leaf quickly through the pages of spells.

'Merlin, it's too dangerous,' Gaius protested.

'We don't have a choice!' said Merlin.

But Gaius knew there was another option.

'Good evening, sire,' the doctor said with a bow as he entered the council chambers. 'There is a matter of great urgency which I must discuss with you.'

'Then spit it out,' said Uther.

Gaius did not try to find excuses or soften the blow. Having served the king for more than twenty years, he had earned the right to speak plainly. Although he still, at times, had to accept the consequences of doing so.

'Tristan's tomb is empty,' he told the king. 'I believe he has been conjured from the dead, as a wraith. He has come to take vengeance for Ygraine's death.'

'It was magic that killed her, not I!' Uther cried.

'Nevertheless, it was you he blamed,' said Gaius calmly. 'You cannot allow Arthur to fight. No weapon forged by man can kill a wraith. It will stop at nothing until it has accomplished what it came for. Arthur cannot win; he will die.'

'He will not listen to me,' said the king, sounding as hopeless as Gaius had ever heard him.

The physician paused before answering. This was one of those times when the consequences of his words might be unpleasant. 'Then you must tell him who the knight is,' he said. 'You cannot hide the truth for ever.'

Uther turned on him in fury. 'I am the king! You will not tell me what I can and cannot do!'

But Gaius would not allow the king to

intimidate him. 'That is your choice, sire,' he said. 'You tell him, or let him go to his death. But the boy is of age: he should know.'

The king's voice was threatening. 'No one but you and I will ever know the secret of Arthur's birth. You made an oath. I warn you not to break it.'

Gaius knew he could push the king no further. 'Very well, sire,' he said at last.

'Leave me,' the king snapped, and Gaius had no choice but to go. He only hoped that Uther would think over his words and take action.

Outside the castle, the Black Knight stood unmoving in front of the gates of Camelot.

Towards him crept a much smaller figure with magic in mind.

Merlin took a deep breath, raised his hand towards the knight and began speaking the language of magic. A path of

flame shot out from him and surrounded the stranger in a fiery ring. The flames billowed higher, engulfing the knight – surely they would consume him!

But as the fire died down, Merlin was astonished to see that the wraith still stood there. No mortal weapon could kill it, and now it seemed as if magic couldn't harm it either.

The knight suddenly turned his head in Merlin's direction and the boy took to his heels in panic.

CHAPTER THIRTEEN

NIMUEH'S REVENGE

Merlin wasn't just running to get away from the knight. He needed to see Arthur straight away. His plan had failed and he didn't have another one – the only thing he could possibly do now was persuade the prince not to fight.

He burst into Arthur's room, finding the prince practising his sword strokes.

'Merlin, you know that conversation we had about knocking—' the prince began wearily, but Merlin immediately interrupted him.

'You have to pull out,' he said.

'And why's that?'

'Because he'll kill you!' Merlin cried.

Arthur seemed irritated. 'Why does everybody think that?'

'Because they're right!' Merlin took a deep breath. 'Just pull out. You're the Crown Prince. No one wants to see you die over some stupid challenge.'

'I'm *not* a coward,' the prince told him.

How to make him understand? How to make him see this was a matter of life and death? 'I know that. I've stood here and watched you overcome every fear you've ever faced. But you are more than that. You are not merely a warrior, you are a prince. A future king. You have proved your courage, but you must prove your wisdom.'

Arthur didn't even look at him. 'I'm not backing down.'

'Please, Arthur, listen to me!' Merlin went over to the window, gesturing down at the gates where the wraith still stood. 'This is no ordinary knight! Look at him – he doesn't eat, he doesn't sleep, he just stands there in total silence. Doesn't that tell you something?'

The prince didn't even glance out of the window. 'No one is unbeatable.'

'If you fight him, you will die,' Merlin said.

'I'm not listening to this,' Arthur replied.

Merlin shouted in desperation, 'I'm trying to warn you, Arthur!'

'And I'm warning you, Merlin!' The furious prince turned on his servant and Merlin jumped hurriedly out of the way of his sword.

There was nothing more he could do. He turned and left the room.

★

Uther was alone in the council chamber – or so he thought. A sudden breeze whisked through the room and the king turned his head as the candles were extinguished. When he turned back again, a young woman was standing before him.

Uther had not seen Nimueh for many years, and this woman was far too young to be the sorceress he'd known. But Gaius had told him of the disguise she was now adopting, and the brilliant blue eyes seemed very familiar to him. The king had no doubt of her identity – and suddenly realized he was not surprised to see her here. 'I should have known...' he whispered.

She smiled in delight. 'It is more than I'd hoped for, Uther. Soon Arthur will be slain. You will have sent him to his death.'

SOON ARTHUR WILL BE SLAIN. YOU HAVE SENT HIM TO HIS DEATH.

'Haven't you tired of revenge?' Uther asked her.

'Haven't you?' Her smile vanished. 'You began this war when you threw me from the court and slaughtered all of my kind!'

'You brought it on yourselves,' Uther insisted. 'You practised evil.'

Nimueh stared at him in disbelief. 'I was your friend, Uther! You welcomed me here and I did as you asked – I used the magic you so despise to give your barren wife the son you craved!'

'Don't ever speak of her in that way,' said the king in a low voice. 'She was my heart. My soul. And you took her from me!'

'She died giving birth to your son! It was not my choice. That is the law of magic. To create a life, there had to be a death.' For a second she looked almost sad. 'The balance of the world had to be repaid.'

'You knew it would kill her,' Uther said.

'No,' she replied, 'you're wrong. If I had foreseen her death and the terrible retribution you would seek . . . I would never have granted your wish.'

Uther's ancient grief threatened to overwhelm him. 'I wish you hadn't,' he said.

'You wish you didn't have a son?' Suddenly her smile was back. 'Well, your wish will come true tomorrow.'

'I will not let you take him,' said the king.

Nimueh fixed Uther with a vengeful stare. 'I have watched so many people I love die at your hands, Uther Pendragon. Now it is your turn.'

Uther looked away in despair. When he turned back, she had gone.

CHAPTER FOURTEEN
AN OLD STORY

After so many failures, most people would have given up. Not Merlin. Arthur's obstinacy had made him even more determined to help because it had shown him that nothing would dissuade the prince from fighting the Black Knight.

One thing he had learned from Gaius was that there was much wisdom to be found in books. Gaius' many volumes hadn't helped, but there was a chamber in the palace where even more books could be found: the Hall of Records.

It was night, so the door was locked, but that was no obstacle to Merlin – yet another example of how handy magic could be. He began to search through the shelves, starting with the dustiest and most neglected – on the assumption that tomes about defeating wraiths wouldn't be the most commonly consulted, especially in a land where magic was banned. It seemed an almost hopeless task, though – among these thousands of books, how could he possibly hope to find the right one, if there even *was* a right one, and before noon the next day? – but he had to try; he had no other ideas.

A cobwebbed book slipped from his hands and he knelt down to pick it up. He stood up again – and found himself looking into the angry face of Geoffrey of Monmouth.

'How did you get in here?' demanded the records keeper.

'The door was open,' Merlin told him. Well, it wasn't exactly a lie. The door *was* open – after Merlin had magically opened it.

'And you thought you'd come in and help yourself?' the man said, staring pointedly at the book in Merlin's hand.

Merlin's instinct was to try to bluff his way out of the situation. But as he opened his mouth to tell some plausible story, he stopped. This man knew all about books, and he was a friend of Gaius'. This could be Merlin's biggest stroke of luck yet!

So he told the truth. 'Gaius thinks the Black Knight is a wraith,' he said. 'Arthur's in mortal peril. I was looking for something to help. I need to find a weapon that will kill something that's already dead.'

The old man nodded his understanding. 'Ah yes, I have read of such things in the ancient chronicles.'

Merlin stared at him in amazement. 'Really? What did they say?'

'Several old stories — fables — speak of ancient swords—'

'That can kill the dead?' Merlin interrupted.

Geoffrey nodded again. 'The swords the fables speak of can destroy anything — alive or dead.'

This was all that Merlin had hoped for! 'Can you show me one of these fables?' he asked urgently.

'Well, let me think . . .' Geoffrey seemed to

take for ever to consider the matter, and Merlin fought to keep his impatience under control. Finally the record keeper turned and went over to a shelf. Oh, so slowly, he sorted through a pile of books and scrolls until he eventually found the one he wanted. 'This is *The Chronicle of Beltain*,' he told Merlin, who was fighting a desire to yell *Hurry up! Hurry up!* at the old man.

Geoffrey turned over the pages, examining each one carefully. In the end he stopped and began to read. 'Ah, here we are. "Sir Marhaus looked upon the great sword begotten in the Dragon's breath and found it passing good—"'

'What did you say?' Merlin demanded. He stared down at the open book. There was a picture of a very familiar creature, breathing fire onto a glowing sword.

'"The great sword begotten in the Dragon's breath . . ."' repeated Geoffrey. But Merlin didn't wait to hear any more. He had got exactly what he came for. All he needed now was a Dragon – and a sword.

Merlin wasn't the only person in the palace hatching plots to try to save Arthur. The Lady Morgana, beset by strange forebodings, had begged the prince to abandon the fight. And the king himself, terrified by Nimueh's visit, had finally come to a decision.

Gaius, preparing for bed in his chambers, was surprised when the door opened and Uther walked in. He was even more surprised when the king's first words were, 'I'm sorry.' Uther came further into the room. 'You knew that one day this business would come back to haunt me,' he continued.

'Not quite so literally,' said Gaius.

'I should have listened to you. You said that no good would come of using witch-craft at Arthur's birth.'

Gaius was in no mood to argue with the king over things long since past. 'You wanted an heir,' he said. 'You thought it was the only way.'

'Nimueh told me there would be a price to pay,' said Uther.

'You weren't to know that the price would be Ygraine's life.'

Both physician and king fell silent, thinking of that terrible time.

Finally Uther spoke. 'I cannot let Arthur die.'

'Then you must stop the fight,' Gaius said.

'No,' the king replied. 'I will take his place.'

The doctor stared at Uther in shock. 'Do you know what you're saying?'

I CANNOT LET ARTHUR DIE... I WILL TAKE HIS PLACE.

But it was clear that the king knew only too well. 'Ygraine gave up her life for him; so must I. I have no other choice. My death will stop the wraith and Arthur will live.' He gazed at Gaius – a look that was almost pleading rather than commanding. 'It means that you will be the only person left who knows the truth about Arthur's birth. I want

you to swear to me that you will keep
your oath.'

Finally Gaius nodded. He did not
agree with the king; he thought Arthur
should know the truth. But he was the
king's faithful servant, and he must do
this thing that was asked of him. As
far as it was in his power to grant, he
must let Uther go to his death in
peace. 'I will take the secret to my grave,'
he said.

Uther's relief was clear. He placed a
hand on Gaius' shoulder. 'You've always
been a good friend,' he said, 'despite my
temper.'

They both managed a weak smile. 'I always thought that would be the death of you,' the physician replied.

He waited for the king to take his leave, but Uther had not yet finished. 'I have one other favour to ask,' he began . . .

Chapter Fifteen

Dragon Fire

Merlin hurried through the palace, clutching a long, thin bundle wrapped in a blanket. He didn't want anyone to wonder why he was wandering around in the middle of the night with Tom the blacksmith's best sword.

Gwen had been surprised when Merlin came to ask for the strongest sword her father had ever made; she was reluctant to hand it over without Tom's permission. 'He's been saving it,' she'd said. 'He'll kill me if he finds I've taken it.' But after Merlin explained that it was to save Arthur, she had made no further protest.

Now Merlin just needed the second ingredient from the fable – the Dragon.

Finally he reached the deep vaults where the Great Dragon was held prisoner. The huge creature flew down to greet him.

'Do you know why I'm here?' Merlin asked.

'It may surprise you, Merlin, but my knowledge of your life is not universal,' the Dragon replied.

Actually it did surprise him – before, the Dragon had always seemed to know more about Merlin's life than he did himself.

He hurried to explain. 'It's to do with Arthur: his life's in danger. He has to fight a wraith. He will die – unless I can make a weapon that will kill the dead.' He knelt down to unwrap the sword. 'Will you burnish this, to save Arthur?'

To his amazement, the sword spun out of his hands, floating through the air to hang before the Dragon. The creature considered it for a while before saying, 'The dead do not return without reason. Who has he come for?'

'Uther,' Merlin said.

'Then let him take his vengeance and the wraith will die without my aid.'

Merlin should have known that the Dragon would feel like that − after all, Uther was the one who had imprisoned it here − but it didn't understand the full story. 'It's Arthur who's going to fight the wraith, though. You have to save him.'

'That is *your* destiny, young warlock, not mine,' the Dragon told him.

Merlin was frustrated. Of course it was his destiny − and he was trying to fulfil it!

He just needed some help to do so. The Dragon had always seemed very keen on Arthur reaching the throne. 'If Arthur fights the wraith and dies, Camelot will have no heir,' he tried. 'I will have no destiny.'

The creature seemed to accept that. 'A weapon forged with my assistance will have great power,' it pointed out.

'I know—' Merlin began, but he was interrupted.

'You do not know,' the Dragon said. 'You can only guess. You have not seen what I have seen. If you had, perhaps you would not ask this of me. In the wrong hands this sword could do great evil. It must be wielded by Arthur and him alone.'

'I understand,' Merlin said.

'You must do more than understand,' it insisted. 'You must promise.'

Merlin would agree to anything if only the Dragon would help. 'I promise.'

The Dragon raised its head, and the sword floated higher. Merlin ducked back as the creature exhaled, but the heat from its flaming breath still nearly knocked him over. The sword was bathed from hilt to tip in golden, magical fire.

The flames died away but the sword still glowed with a golden fire all of its own. It was the most perfect weapon Merlin had ever seen – the most perfect weapon he could imagine ever existing. He watched in awe as it floated back towards him.

'Heed my words,' the

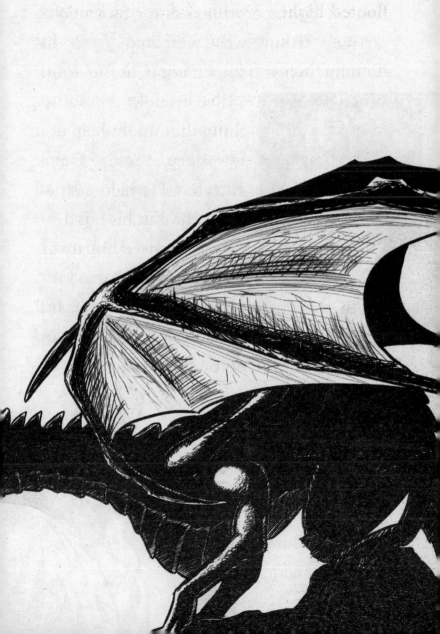

Outside the palace, the Black Knight waited by the castle gates for morning to arrive. Arthur was watching from his window when a knock came at the door.

'I've brought you something that might help you to sleep,' said Gaius, entering. He held a small glass phial in his hand.

Arthur waved him away. 'I'm fine. I don't need it.'

But the doctor was insistent. 'Here. It'll relax you, take the edge off your nerves.' He held out the bottle temptingly.

The prince gave in, grimacing as he swallowed the potion. 'I wouldn't drink it for pleasure!' he exclaimed.

Gaius pointed him towards the bed. 'Why don't you sit down for a moment?'

Arthur was already reeling by the time he made it across the room. 'Mind you,' he said as he sank down on the bed, 'if you forget about the taste ... the after-effect is ... quite pleasurable ...' His eyes closed.

Gaius waited a few moments to make sure the prince was really asleep and then left, locking the door behind him.

The king's wishes had been carried out.

CHAPTER SIXTEEN

THE PLAN UNRAVELS

Merlin was in the armoury well before noon, making sure that all Arthur's armour was in perfect condition. They might have the sword, but Arthur still had to hold off the Black Knight long enough to land a killing blow.

The sword itself lay on a bench, wrapped once again in a blanket to hide it from prying eyes. But now its time had come. Merlin unfolded the covering, gazing reverently at the shimmering blade. Something caught his eye – there were runes engraved on the metal: they hadn't been there before he'd taken the sword to the Dragon. But there was no time to examine them now – the door to the armoury was opening.

He turned, expecting to see Arthur. But instead it was the king himself who entered the room – and what was even more surprising, he was dressed in chain mail as if ready for battle.

Uther's eyes were immediately drawn to the sword. 'That's a fine blade,' he said.

Merlin fought an urge to hide it from the king. Even without the Dragon's warning, he knew that it was Arthur's sword; he felt that no man should see it before the prince. But he dared not offend the king. 'It's for Arthur,' he said.

'He won't be needing it today,' Uther

replied. 'I will be taking his place. Prepare me for battle.'

'But, sire,' Merlin said, his anxiety giving him the courage to speak up against the king, 'Arthur should be the one who fights today.'

'No, the grievance was with me; the fight is mine.'

The circumstances were so strange as to be almost laughable. Here was the king, that ruthless, confident man, so solemn and so distant now, confiding in a lowly servant. A servant who had once nearly died thanks to Uther's cruelty. Merlin did not hate Uther, though. He saw in front of him a man who was walking knowingly to his doom, and he pitied him.

'I'll get your sword,' Merlin said.

But Uther was already reaching out for the Dragon-fired blade. 'This one will be fine.'

The warlock was horrified. 'No, sire, you don't understand – that one was made specifically for Arthur. You'd be better off with a sword you trust.'

But the king seemed fascinated by the sword, almost hypnotized. 'It's worthy of a king. It has almost perfect balance . . . Who made it?'

'Er . . . Tom the blacksmith,' Merlin answered. He was desperately trying to think of a way to prevent the king from using the weapon, but no answer presented itself. He could not take it from the king physically. Nor could he tell the king the truth.

'Tom is not the royal swordsmith,' said Uther. 'I'm surprised Arthur went to him.'

Merlin fetched the king's breastplate, his mind still racing. 'Oh, that was me. I felt he needed a better sword,'

 he added, trying to sound plausible.

Uther seemed even more surprised at that. 'You show him the most extraordinary loyalty.'

'That is my job, sire,' the warlock said.

'But you go beyond the line of duty,' said the king.

'Well ...' said Merlin, not sure how to answer. Almost to his own surprise, he heard himself being honest, confiding in the king as the king had confided in him. 'You could say there's a bond between us.'

'I'm glad.' Uther looked at Merlin, and

he had the strangest feeling that the king was seeing him for the first time as a person, not just a servant. 'Look after him.'

Grasping the sword tightly, Uther Pendragon walked away. He left a very worried young man behind him.

CHAPTER SEVENTEEN
EXCALIBUR

The crowd stared in astonishment as King Uther strode into the tournament ground. The king had been a great warrior but his battles had been won many years before. Now it was Arthur who led the knights into combat, and most people had never seen Uther fight.

Morgana exchanged a look of horror with Gwen. Only Gaius, waiting beside the arena, was unsurprised – and it was he alone who understood Uther's words to the

Black Knight: 'You can have what you came for – the father, not the son.'

At that moment the king's son was still deeply asleep. But slowly, sounds began to rouse him from his drugged slumber – clashing swords, shouting crowds. Still barely conscious, he staggered over to the window to find out what was going on.

As he realized, all drowsiness fled. He ran to the door, but found it locked. He kicked, punched, shouted – all to no avail.

The fight continued without him.

Although Uther had not gone into battle for years, his skill hadn't left him. Arthur might be the greatest warrior in Camelot, but the watching crowd soon saw where his abilities had come from.

Never had it been clearer that this was a

fight to the death. Each stroke was delivered with greater force and speed than the last, the blades little more than glittering blurs in the sunlight.

The king swung round, the mystical sword flying, but the Black Knight blocked it with his own weapon. As he forced it down, Uther swept up with

his shield arm – and the knight's helmet went flying.

There were screams from the crowd. Now they could all see that Uther's opponent was no living man. The wraith's ravaged black flesh clung tight to his skull, his eyes were sightless sockets. His lips were pulled back to reveal rotting teeth. Only Uther and Gaius could see the traces of a man they'd once known beneath the dead mask, and for them that made the sight even more horrific.

Only Uther and Gaius – and one other. A figure had appeared at the back of the crowd, and was watching the fight with fanatical zeal. Nimueh.

The king froze as he took in the reality of what he was facing, but only for a second. The fight began again, its intensity even greater than before. But the shock had shaken Uther. He was being beaten back now, and the watchers gasped as the Black Knight knocked him off balance. The king stumbled backwards, his sword falling from his hand.

Nimueh smiled triumphantly as the crowd gasped, waiting for the killing blow that must follow.

The wraith chopped down like an executioner.

The crowd gasped again – this time in amazement. Uther had raised his shield at the last moment and the Black Knight had swung his sword with such force that it had actually pierced it! The blade was stuck!

The wraith struggled to free his sword, pulling it backwards – and Uther kicked the shield away with all the strength he could muster. Now it was the Black Knight who stumbled. The king grabbed his own sword and thrust forward ...

The sword pierced the wraith's chest. For a moment he looked unconcerned. Then he roared ...

Flames sprang up where the blade had entered. As the Black Knight screamed with rage and disbelief, the fire spread, consuming the rotten flesh.

From the crowd, Nimueh watched, furious, as her champion exploded into dust and her moment of triumph died with him.

The force of the blast knocked Uther off his feet, but he rose again to the cheers of his people.

'I thought you said a wraith couldn't be killed,' the king said later as Gaius tended his wounds.

'Yes, it was remarkable,' the physician agreed. He pointed to where Uther's blade lay. 'Is that a new sword, sire?'

The king nodded. 'It's the best I've ever fought with.' He reached over and picked it up. 'Have a look. I was intrigued by those markings.'

Gaius examined the runes. 'On one side it says *Take me up*, and on the other *Cast me away*.'

'What does that mean?' asked the king.

But Gaius didn't answer. Instead he enquired, 'May I ask who made it, sire?'

'Merlin gave it to me,' the king said. 'It was forged for Arthur.'

He didn't noticed Gaius' look – at once understanding and amazed. Because at that moment the doors were flung open and a furious Prince Arthur stormed in.

Gaius retreated quickly, leaving father and son alone.

Arthur had been boiling with fury ever since a cringing servant had released him from his room. His only thought was how little faith his father must have in him to prevent him from fighting, and how much contempt he must have to disgrace him so. For years the king had belittled him, punished him, refused to listen to or understand him, but this was a greater insult than he'd ever known before.

'You had Gaius drug me!' the prince roared. 'I was *meant* to fight him!'

'No,' said the king. 'You weren't.'

'But the knight's code—'

'The knight's code be damned.' Uther did not shout back at his son, but the passion in his voice was unmistakable nonetheless. 'I believed you would die. And that was a risk I could not take. You are too precious to me. You mean more to me than anything I know. More than this entire kingdom – and certainly more than my own life.'

Arthur stared at the king in shock. Never in his life had he dreamed that his father felt this way. He could barely take it in. 'I . . . always thought that – that I was a big

disappointment to you,' he managed at last.

'Well, that is my fault and not yours,' said Uther. He put his hand on the boy's shoulder. 'You are my only son, and I wouldn't wish for another.'

It was more than Arthur could deal with. His beliefs had been turned upside down in a moment, and the love he saw in his father's eyes was something wonderful and strange. He looked away. He would need to think about this later; it was too much for now. He searched for something to say – something that might acknowledge Uther's words but take him away from them too. 'I heard you fought pretty well,' he said after a moment.

The king smiled. 'Thanks.'

'You should join us for training. Sort out

your footwork.'

'I'll show you footwork!' Laughing, Uther rose and aimed a playful kick at his son, who dodged out of the way and headed for the door.

As Arthur left, he realized he hadn't heard his father laugh like that for a very long time.

CHAPTER EIGHTEEN
CAST ME AWAY

Gaius and Merlin were having supper together. The young warlock was trying hard to ignore Gaius' questioning gaze.

'You know why I'm looking at you,' the physician said at last.

'No,' Merlin replied untruthfully.

'Uther told me you provided him with his sword today.' Merlin didn't answer. 'It must be a very powerful blade to slay the dead. Did you enchant it?'

'No.' Merlin wasn't entirely sure why he didn't confide in Gaius, except that he'd never told the doctor that he visited the Dragon and was a bit worried how he'd react. Oh, and Gaius could get so cross when he used magic, even when it turned out all right. Not that this had turned out all right exactly. Arthur was alive and the wraith was gone, but Merlin's promise to the Dragon had been broken and he didn't want to think about what that might mean.

'Shame,' Gaius said. 'Whoever did enchant it saved the king's life. I'd have been very proud of you.'

Merlin hastily reconsidered. He didn't have to tell Gaius *everything* and a bit of praise would be very nice. 'Well . . .' he said.

'Never mind,' said Gaius dismissively. 'If it wasn't you, it wasn't you.'

But as the doctor turned back to his food, Merlin spotted that he was not quite hiding a smile.

Gaius' reaction had cheered up Merlin so much that his concerns about the sword had slipped from his mind. But they came back with a rush when he woke in the night to hear a voice calling his name – a voice inside his head. The Great Dragon was summoning him.

He hurried down to the vaults with a feeling of dread. Maybe it wouldn't be so bad. The Dragon would surely understand that Merlin hadn't broken his promise deliberately, and Uther would probably just put the sword away somewhere and forget about it. It wasn't as if the king was likely to go around doing 'great evil' with it.

'So, does Arthur live?' the creature boomed

as Merlin hurried towards it.

'Yes,' he said. 'The sword worked, it was incredible, amazing ... But ...'

'Yes?'

The warlock took a deep breath. 'Things didn't quite go according to plan. I mean, they did, except ... it wasn't Arthur who wielded the sword. It was Uther.'

The Great Dragon screamed.

Merlin took a step back, scared by the force of the Dragon's rage. He stammered out an explanation as it soared into the air, still screaming. 'I tried – I couldn't stop him – he's the king ...'

The creature flew back down at last. Merlin had never felt so small in front of the huge beast. 'The sword was born of the old magic,' the Dragon roared. 'You have no idea of its power. In the hands of Uther it will bring only evil.'

'I'll get it back!' Merlin cried.

But it was not to be that easy. 'You have betrayed me,' said the Dragon. 'You are not ready to be trusted.'

He tried again. 'I'll bring it to you. You can destroy it.'

'What is made cannot be unmade,' the creature said. It was an odd thing to say, but Merlin thought he knew what the Dragon meant. Once magic had brought a thing into the world, it was there to stay.

'So what do you want me to do?' he asked.

'Take the sword far from here and place it where no mortal man can ever find it,' the Dragon said. Then it flew away without another word, leaving behind a worried and scared warlock. Merlin was beginning to realize just how terrible sorcery could be. Not just for the things it could do, but for the prices it demanded in return – and the consequences that might come of a broken promise.

The sword was in the armoury, just stuck in a rack as if it were any old weapon. Merlin took it out reverently. This time he was able to study the runes properly. *Take me up . . . Cast me away.* Well, that was what he must do – cast it away.

He wrapped it up in a blanket once more and set off.

Many miles from Camelot there was a lake – an isolated, lonely spot. Here, surely, was a place where no man could ever find the sword.

Merlin drew it from its covering. The blade glinted in the sunlight, looking for a moment as if the Dragon's fire were still on it. As he gazed at it, Merlin felt suddenly that this was Arthur's sword – it had been made for him, it was his. He had a desperate urge to ride back to the castle and present the blade to the prince. Surely Arthur would use it to do great things.

But with his broken promise, Merlin had forfeited the right to decide the sword's fate.

With sudden resolve, he hurled it from him. It twisted over and over in the air and cut the water with barely a splash – then sank out of sight.

Merlin turned away. But he could not rid himself of the idea that Arthur was meant to wield that sword.

Perhaps, somehow, one day, the sword would find its way back to its true master.

ALSO AVAILABLE

THE MAGIC
BEGINS

Text by
Jacqueline Rayner

Based on the stories by Julian Jones
and Howard Overman

Continue the adventures at
bbc.co.uk/**merlin**

CHAPTER ONE

CAMELOT!

Merlin reached the top of a hill and stopped. He'd been walking for hours and was tired, but he couldn't stop smiling — because finally the castle lay before him. Camelot! He stood and gazed down in wonder.

Merlin had hardly ever left the small village where he'd been born. He'd certainly never visited anywhere half as grand as Camelot, the amazing castle of King Uther that contained an entire city. It looked even more incredible than he'd imagined – the vast stone walls, the imposing battlements, the majestic turrets. And he was going to live there!

His mother, Hunith, had written a letter to the king's doctor, Gaius, asking him to look after her son. It wasn't that Merlin couldn't take care of himself – Hunith knew that he could. In fact, that was what worried her. The problem was, Merlin was . . . special.

Even Merlin didn't know quite how special he was. But someone – some*thing* – knew. A very old and powerful something that was waiting in Camelot for the boy to arrive. Before long, Merlin would meet the one who had been calling to him, and make some incredible discoveries about his own future.

But for now, never imagining what lay ahead of him, he shrugged his pack higher onto his shoulders, took a last look at the view behind him – where, if he squinted, he imagined he could still see the speck of Ealdor, his old village – and set off once more on his journey.

The hustle and bustle, the colours, the noise! Never had a place felt so alive. Nobody spared a glance for the dark-haired youth who stepped through the gates of Camelot many hours later, but Merlin didn't care. Why should they look at him when there was so much else to see? He laughed happily, the sound swallowed up in the hubbub of the city. Then suddenly, underneath the shouting and laughter and children's cries, he heard the *thump thump thump* of a drum.

Merlin pushed his way through the crowds, eager to see what was happening.

He was near the heart of the city now, the king's palace. Could that be ...Yes! Coming out onto the balcony, the king himself, Uther Pendragon. But Merlin hadn't imagined that the lord of such a lively city would look so harsh.

He soon discovered the reason for the king's displeasure.

Guards dressed in chain mail led forward a peasant. The man's hands were tied behind him, and he looked exhausted and hopeless.

King Uther began to address the crowd. "Let this serve as a lesson to

AT THE CITY GATES . . .

all," he said. "This man, Thomas James Collins, is judged guilty of conspiring to use enchantments and magic. Such practices are banned, on penalty of death."

The man had been condemned to death – for using magic! The smile left Merlin's face. Suddenly his new life in Camelot no longer seemed like an exciting adventure. It was dangerous here.

Thomas Collins was led up onto a raised platform, where a man with an axe stood waiting for him. Merlin knew what was going to happen next.

He saw the king's arm come

down sharply, the signal for the axeman's arm to do the same, and he turned away. But he couldn't block out the swish of the blade – or the thud that followed it.

The sound had scarcely died away when Uther began speaking again. "When I came to this land, this kingdom was mired in chaos. But with the people's help, magic was driven from the realm. So I declare a festival – to celebrate twenty years since the Great Dragon was captured and Camelot freed from the evil of sorcery." The king was no longer stern. He smiled, inviting the people to join in the celebration.

But Merlin did not feel like celebrating – and he was not alone.

The crowd parted to let through an old woman. She lifted a tear-stained face to the king and cried: "There is only one evil in this land and it is not magic — it is *you*!"

"Mary, no!" came a voice from the crowd, but the woman was too upset to take any notice.

"You took my son, and I promise you — before these celebrations are over, you will share my tears." Her gaze flicked to the axeman's block before returning to Uther. "An eye for an eye, a tooth for a tooth — a son for a son!"

"Seize her!" cried the king. His guards ran forward as he shouted, but they were too late. Mary grabbed the pendant around her neck and muttered a spell.

The pendant glowed. Suddenly a whirlwind sprang up from nowhere. For a second it was impossible to tell where the woman ended and the tornado began, and then, in an instant, both were gone, leaving nothing but a few floating leaves as evidence of their presence.

Merlin looked back at the king. This was sorcery, and the boy could tell that Uther would make no allowances for a mother's grief. The woman had signed her own death warrant with her spell. That was what magic led to in this land. Merlin lowered his eyes quickly, suddenly anxious that the king might meet his gaze, pick him out of all the people in the crowd, realize what he was.

Worried and nervous, Merlin made his way through the crowd. He didn't think they'd seen the last of Mary Collins, and he wondered what exactly her threat meant.

ALSO AVAILABLE

POTIONS AND POISON

A deadly plague is sweeping through
Camelot and Gwen is accused of witchcraft.

Somehow Merlin must find a cure and
save his friend from execution, but before
long Merlin finds his own life in danger!
Prince Arthur tries to help, but it seems
he may be walking into a trap . . .

978 0 553 82112 3

ALSO AVAILABLE

A FIGHTING CHANCE

Merlin wants to help his new friend,
Lancelot, become a Knight of Camelot
– but it's not as easy as he hopes.

Then the Lady Morgana is struck down by
a mystery illness. Gaius is baffled and a new
physician arrives to help. He seems to have
all the answers, but Merlin suspects that
there's something sinister going on.

978 0 553 82501 5

ALSO AVAILABLE

MERLIN: THE COMPLETE GUIDE

Explore Merlin's world and find out all there is to know about the characters and their secrets. With facts and great imagery of all the cast, locations and props. Discover the lore and legend of Merlin!

Never seen before footage as well as maps and spells from the spell book finish this complete guide. It's a must have for any Merlin fan!

978 0 553 82108 6

ALSO AVAILABLE

MERLIN MYSTERY ACTIVITY BOOK

A mysterious stranger has taken Arthur
prisoner and Merlin has to find him and
set him free. Join Merlin on a dangerous
journey to save Arthur. Work through the
puzzles, play the games and answer the
riddles to help Merlin save his friend,
the future king of Camelot.

This activity book includes a free
spell notebook!

978 0 553 82105 5

ALSO AVAILABLE

MERLIN QUEST ACTIVITY BOOK

This Quest Activity book sets the stage
for tournament day in Camelot. But
danger lurks around every corner. An evil
knight threatens Arthur, can he defeat him
in battle? Join Arthur and his friends on
their adventure around Camelot. Solve the
puzzles, play the games and answer the
riddles to help Arthur defeat the evil
knight and win the tournament.

This activity book includes a
free pull-out game!

978 0 553 82106 2

THE DRAGON'S CALL

When Merlin arrives in the great kingdom
of Camelot he discovers a dark side to the
bustling city: magic is outlawed on pain of
death! If he wants to stay alive, Merlin will
have to keep his unique magical talents a
closely guarded secret . . .

978 0 553 82109 3

VALIANT

A mysterious new knight arrives in Camelot
for the sword tournament. His fighting skills
are impressive but when an opponent is not
just injured but *poisoned*, Merlin suspects that
dark magic is involved. Merlin is determined
to expose the evil, but Arthur is next in line
to fight and time is running out . . .

978 0 553 82110 9

THE MARK OF NIMUEH

A deadly plague rages through
Camelot and it seems that sorcery is the
only explanation. When Gwen is arrested
for witchcraft, Merlin knows the wrong
person is accused, but can he uncover
the truth, find a cure and save his
friend from execution?

978 0 553 82114 7

ALSO AVAILABLE
FOR OLDER READERS

THE POISONED
CHALICE

Merlin is poisoned by the sorceress
Nimueh and Arthur seeks the only antidote
that can save him – but the prince
is walking into a trap . . .

978 0 553 82115 4